A Very Special Birthday

First published in the UK by HarperCollins Children's Books in 2010

1 3 5 7 9 10 8 6 4 2
ISBN: 978-0-00-733598-5

A Very Special Birthday

HarperCollins *Children's Books*

Whiz and Lindy were hard at
work in the garage when Noddy
and Tessie called by.

"I've been checking my book of Toy Town birthdays and yours isn't in it!" Lindy told Whiz.

"It is because robots do not have birthdays," Whiz explained. "We just have lots and lots of work days."

Noddy didn't think this sounded very fair.
Suddenly, he had an idea.
"Let's make today your birthday!" he cried.

"Oh, that's a great idea!" agreed Tessie.

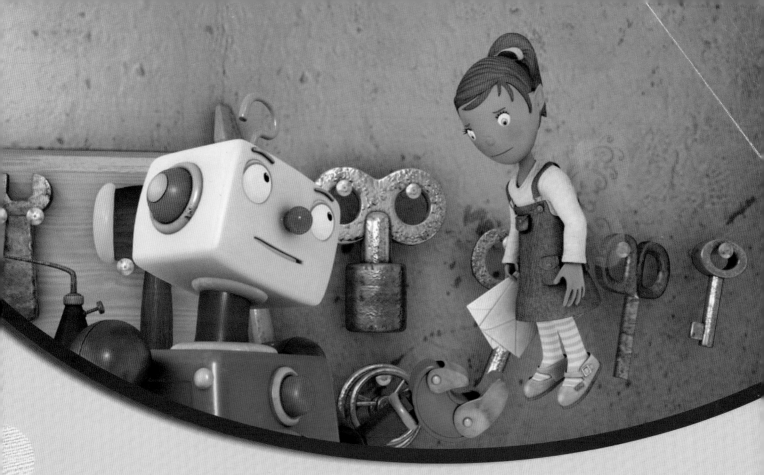

"Beep!"

said Whiz. "Thank you, but what is a birthday?"

Lindy couldn't believe Whiz didn't know! "It's when you get a year older," she explained. "And you get birthday cards and a birthday present!"

9

Whiz thought birthdays sounded lots of fun.

"I feel so happy and excited!" he cried, as he rolled out of the garage and down the street.

"Bzzt!
Buzz!
Beep!"

Everyone was so busy watching Whiz,
they didn't notice the naughty goblins
hiding round the corner.

"There's some horrible birthday
fun going on around here,"
Sly told Gobbo, looking at his funometer.
"And what is goblin rule number one?"

"Always try and spoil the fun!"
Sly and Gobbo cackled together.

Just then, Mr Plod arrived at the garage.
"Now we can play some party games,"
Noddy cheered. "This one's called pass the parcel."

"My favourite!" laughed Mr Plod.

Whiz looked puzzled as the friends passed the parcel. "Nobody seems to like this parcel," he said to Noddy.

"No, Whiz, you're supposed to keep passing it until the music stops!" Noddy chuckled. "Then you unwrap it."

"Oh, I did not know that," Whiz told him.

Sly and Gobbo were still spying on the friends.
"Ha, ha, Whiz doesn't know what to do!" laughed Gobbo.

"Yes, so we could tell him anything," added Sly, with a grin.

When Noddy and the others left the garage
to plan a surprise party for Whiz,
the goblins saw their chance to make mischief!

"Happy birthday!"

Sly cried, as he crept up on Whiz.

"Noddy forgot to tell you about some other important fun things that happen on birthdays."

"When anyone says 'happy birthday' you have to crow like a cockerel," Sly fibbed.

"Cock-a-doodle-do!"

crowed Gobbo.

"And you should eat your birthday cards," added Sly.

"Goodness, I thought we'd be eating party food," said Whiz in surprise.

18

"What about his birthday present, Sly?"
asked Gobbo.

"It's normal to throw it away," said Sly.
"Out to sea if possible!"

Sly nudged Gobbo. "Well, if that doesn't spoil the party,
I don't know what will!" he whispered.

Meanwhile, Noddy, Tessie
and Mr Plod had prepared a lovely birthday
picnic and were waiting for Whiz to come by.

"Surprise!" they shouted out as he passed.

"Happy birthday, Whiz," laughed Noddy.

"Cock-a-doodle-do!"

crowed Whiz.

21

The goblins were watching from behind a bush.

"He did it!"

chuckled Sly. "That will spoil their fun!"

But to Sly's dismay,
Noddy and the others just laughed
and joined in with the crowing!

"Here's your birthday card," said Noddy,
giving Whiz a brightly coloured card.

"Ah, thank you, Noddy," Whiz replied.
"I know exactly what to do with this."

To Noddy's surprise,
Whiz took a great big bite out of it!

"Ta-da!"

Whiz cried, holding the card up in the air.

"A butterfly!" Noddy gasped, looking at the
shape Whiz had bitten. "That's lovely."

The goblins couldn't understand
what was happening.

"Something's wrong, Sly," said Gobbo.
"Every time you try to spoil the fun,
you just make it more fun!"

"Here's your present," said Noddy,
handing Whiz a pretty box.

"What am I supposed to do with my
present?" wondered Whiz.
"Ah yes, I remember!" he said,
throwing the gift into the stream!

"Ha-ha-ha!"

laughed Sly, running over to look at the present.
"I told you I'd spoil their fun!"

"Sorry Sly, you haven't ruined anything," said Noddy,
"because Whiz's birthday present is...

…a remote control boat!"

Everyone laughed as the boat
floated out of the box into the water.
Everyone except the goblins that is!

NODDY
IN TOYLAND®

**Look out for more
Noddy in Toyland books!**

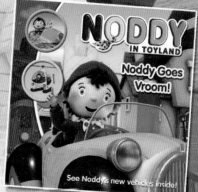

Noddy Goes Vroom!

See Noddy's new vehicles inside!

Noddy and the Pirates

Hide-and-Seek Fun

The Magic Watering Can